Tales from Shakespeare

Julius Caesar

Mark Antony
Caesar's closest friend,
a soldier

Julius Caesar
A rich and successful
soldier and politician

Brutus
A politician and friend
of Caesar

Casca
Conspirator against
Caesar

Trebonius
Conspirator against
Caesar

Octavius
Caesar's great-nephew
and his heir

Calpurnia
Caesar's wife

Cassius
Brother-in-law of
Brutus, leader of
the conspiracy
against Caesar

Portia
Brutus's wife

Decius
Conspirator against
Caesar

**Metellus
Cimber**
Conspirator against
Caesar

Timothy Knapman
Illustrated by Yaniv Shimony

QED Publishing

Triumph and Conspiracy

Act one

The people of Rome loved Julius Caesar. He was a great general and every time he celebrated another victory over his enemies, crowds flocked to cheer him.

Crowds of people clustered around and trumpets blew as Caesar and his friends walked through the city.

As the procession turned a corner, a fortune-teller stepped out of the crowd and went up to Caesar. Everyone was so shocked that they fell silent at once.

"Beware the Ides of March," the old man said.

Like many Romans, Caesar was very superstitious. He stared at the man. What could he mean? What was going to happen on the "Ides" – the 15th of March?

Then Caesar recovered himself. "What nonsense!" he said. Soldiers pushed the old man out of the way and Caesar moved on to the Forum, the great square at the heart of the city.

Two of his party were left behind. One was Brutus, a dear friend of Caesar, and the other his brother-in-law, Cassius.

"You seem troubled," said Cassius.
"These are bad times," said Brutus.
Suddenly, they heard a shout from
the Forum. Then another, and another.

Brutus frowned. "I'm
afraid the people want to
make Caesar king," he said.
"The fools have
forgotten their history,"
said Cassius. "Hundreds of
years ago, we drove out the
last Roman king – the evil
tyrant Tarquin. Ever since,
we Romans have been free
men. If they make Caesar
king, we will all become his
slaves. We can't allow that to happen."
"What are you
suggesting?" said Brutus.
"Your ancestor
helped to overthrow King
Tarquin," said Cassius.

The fault, dear
Brutus, is not in
our stars, but in
ourselves that we
are underlings
– Cassius

Cassius has a lean and hungry look; He thinks too much; such men are dangerous
    – *Caesar*

"Now it's your turn to end a tyranny, before it takes root."

Before Brutus could answer, Caesar and his party returned.

"Look at Cassius," Caesar whispered to his friend Mark Antony. "I don't trust him. He's too thin. Contented men relax and get fat, but not him – he thinks too much. I worry he's plotting against me."

"You have nothing to fear from him, Caesar," chuckled Antony. "Men who think too much are no good in a fight." And the two men walked off.

Casca was about to follow them when Cassius stopped him.

"What happened in the Forum?" said Cassius.

"Brutus and I heard three shouts."

"Antony offered Caesar a crown three times," said Casca, "But each time Caesar refused it."

"What did the crowd do?" asked Cassius.

"They begged him to take it," said Casca.

Cassius looked at Brutus. "What did I tell you?" he said.

That night there was a terrible storm. Casca was running home through the rain when he bumped into Cassius.

"What's the matter with you?" Cassius asked. "You're shaking like a leaf!"

"This storm is a very bad omen," said Casca. "The gods are angry."

"What is wrong with Romans these days?" said Cassius. "We used to be brave and strong but now we're frightened of everything – even the weather! No wonder you bow before a man no better than you."

"Do you mean Caesar?" asked Casca.

"You know who I mean," said Cassius.

"The rumour is that Caesar is going to the Senate tomorrow," said Casca. "They're going to make him king. Then we will all be his subjects."

"I'd rather kill myself," said Cassius. "Or him."

A jagged fork of lightning flashed in the sky overhead and the thunder crashed, but this time Casca didn't flinch.

"I've been waiting for someone to say that," he said.

"Then you'll join us?" said Cassius. The men shook hands. "We aren't many, but we are all determined to end this threat to our republic... or die trying!"

Omens and Nightmares

Act two

It wasn't the storm that kept Brutus awake that night, but his thoughts. For hundreds of years Rome had been a republic, governed not by one ruler, but by a council called the Senate. Brutus was descended from one of the heroes who made Rome a republic. The freedoms they had fought for had to be preserved.

If there was any chance of Caesar becoming king and ending the republic, Brutus would have to kill him.

But Caesar was his friend. He wouldn't become a tyrant, would he? Brutus couldn't be sure. Having power changed people – he knew that. And if Caesar became king he would have absolute power over Rome and all her Empire.

He would be crown'd:
How that might change his nature,
there's the question
— *Brutus*

Before Brutus could think any further, his slave came in.

"Master," he said, "I don't wish to disturb you, but these messages have been thrown in through the window."

The slave handed Brutus a handful of rolled-up papers. Brutus opened the first one and read:

"You have been sleeping while Rome is in danger."

There was a knock at the door.

"It's Cassius," said the slave, "and some other men."

Brutus knew why they were here. It was time to decide: was he going to join them or not?

"Show them in," he said.

The men came in shaking rain from their cloaks.

'Brutus, thou sleep'st. Awake, and see thyself'
– Letter

"Brutus," said Cassius, "this is Metellus Cimber, Casca, Trebonius and Decius."

"Welcome," said Brutus. "Let's join hands."

"Are we going to swear an oath?" asked Cassius.

"We don't need to," said Brutus, "we are honourable Romans and we know this thing must be done."

Conspiracy, shamest thou to show thy dangerous brow by night, when evils are most free?
– *Brutus*

"But tell us," said Decius. "Is it only Caesar who must die?"

"A good question," said Cassius. "His friend Mark Antony is a great warrior and very loyal to him. If we don't kill him too, he's sure to come after us wanting revenge."

"No," said Brutus, "it will look bad. We have to kill Caesar or he'll become a tyrant. If we start slaughtering his friends as well, people will think we're just a bunch of murderers. When Caesar's gone, Antony will have no power anyway. He'll be no threat to us."

Let us be sacrificers, but not butchers
– Brutus

"Very well," said Cassius. "We'll do it tomorrow, when Caesar is on his way to the Senate to be crowned."

At that moment, there was a noise. Brutus nearly jumped out of his skin.

"What was that?" he said, and then realized it was only the clock striking.

"Three o'clock," said Trebonius. "It's time to go, before anyone wakes up. We don't want to be spotted leaving this house."

"But Caesar is a superstitious man," said Decius. "He's bound to be worried by this storm. He might even decide to stay at home tomorrow. I'll go to his house and make sure he comes to the Senate."

"Good man," said Cassius. "Now we should all go and get ready. What is it, Brutus?"

"I've just realized," said Brutus. "Tomorrow is the 15th. The Ides of March."

When the conspirators
had gone, Brutus again
tried to sleep but
couldn't. His wife,
Portia, found him
pacing, lost in thought.

 "What's the
matter?" she asked.
Her voice was weak. She had always been
in poor health. "You're acting very oddly."

 "I'm sorry, my darling," said Brutus.
"I think I must be ill."

 "If you were ill then you'd take
medicine," said Portia. "It's something
else. Tell me, please: I'm your wife and
I love you."

 "I wish I could," said Brutus, but he
turned and walked away.

Caesar couldn't sleep either. As he lay
in bed, his wife, Calpurnia, tossed and
turned beside him.

Suddenly she cried out, "Help! They're murdering Caesar!"

Caesar's blood ran cold. First the fortune-teller's warning and now this! He sent a servant to the temple to ask the priests what the omens were for the day.

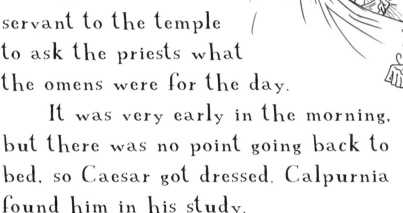

It was very early in the morning, but there was no point going back to bed, so Caesar got dressed. Calpurnia found him in his study.

"I don't care what the priests say," she snapped. "You are not leaving the house! Haven't you heard the rumours? They say graves have opened tonight and the dead have stepped out of them. Blood has dripped from the sky and ghosts have been seen walking the city streets!"

Cowards die many
times before their
deaths, the valiant
taste of death
but once
— Caesar

"I cannot live in fear," said Caesar, trying to convince himself as much as her. "A brave man doesn't waste his days worrying about things that may never happen."

The servant returned from the temple.

"Master," he said, "the priests say the signs are very bad for you; you must stay at home today."

"I'll send Antony in my place," Caesar agreed.

Another slave came in.

"Decius is here to see you, Master," he said.

"Decius, what excellent timing!" said Caesar. "You can go and tell the Senate that I can't see them today after all."

"He's not feeling very well," said Calpurnia.

"No," said Caesar, "I can't lie to them, that would be cowardly. Just tell them I'm not coming."

"But why?" asked Decius. It was his job to make sure Caesar went to the Senate.

"I had a nightmare," Calpurnia explained. "I saw my husband's statue – but it was full of holes. Blood poured from the holes like water from a fountain while people washed their hands in it. Surely that means he is going to be murdered."

Decius knew he had to think quickly.

"You're wrong, my lady," he smiled. "Surely it means that Rome has grown weak, and that the strength that runs in your husband's veins will restore it to health."

"That makes sense," said Caesar, who was easily flattered.

"Besides," said Decius, "I hear they're going to give you a crown. It wouldn't look very good if people found out that you were too frightened to leave your house just because your wife had a bad dream!"

"No it wouldn't!" said Caesar. "See how foolish your worries look now, my dear," he said to Calpurnia with a chuckle.

Before Calpurnia could say anything, Brutus, Casca, Trebonius and Metellus Cimber arrived. A few moments later, Antony joined them.

"Have you all come to accompany me to the Senate?" said Caesar. "Come into the dining room and have some wine. I think we might have something to celebrate today!"

The Ides of March

Act three

As they made their way to the Senate, many people came up to Caesar. Some congratulated him; others asked favours of him. Each time it happened, Cassius felt his stomach lurch. What if someone warned him of their plan?

The Ides of March are come
– *Caesar*
Aye, Caesar, but not gone
– *Fortune-Teller*

When they drew near to the Senate, Trebonius pulled Antony aside and made up a story to distract him. Antony was loyal to Caesar and he was a fierce fighter. The conspirators needed him out of the way.

At last, they drew away from the crowds as they reached the theatre built by Caesar's old rival, Pompey. At the foot of Pompey's statue, Metellus Cimber put his hand on Caesar's arm and begged him to pardon his brother, who had been banished.

"You've asked me this before!" Caesar sighed, exasperated. "The answer is still no! My mind is made up!"

Caesar was so angered by Metellus's pestering that he didn't notice Brutus give a signal to the others. When they drew their daggers and surrounded him, Caesar stared at them for a moment in disbelief.

"What's going on?" he said, and then at last he realized what was happening.

21

Casca struck the
first blow, but the others
quickly followed, stabbing
Caesar over and over again.
Only Brutus held back.
Caesar stood, swaying for a
moment, then Brutus took a deep breath,
walked up to his old friend and drove his
dagger deep into his belly.

"You too, Brutus?" gasped Caesar,
and he fell to the ground, dead.

"Everybody, dip your hands in
Caesar's blood," said Brutus.

Et tu, Brute?
Then fall
Caesar!
— Caesar

"We must show that we are not ashamed of what we've done. We will go to the Forum. There we can explain why we've done this – to free the people from tyranny!"

O mighty Caesar, doth thou lie so low?
– Antony

The others cheered.

Then Mark Antony appeared. He saw Caesar's body and cried out in anguish.

"I can't believe it," he said. "The greatest man of our age and you've killed him!"

"Don't make us kill you too," said Brutus.

Antony could see that Brutus meant it. He put up his hands. "You know me, I'm just a simple soldier," he said.

"I don't know anything about politics.
If you did this, Brutus, I'm sure you had
good reason."

"We did," said Brutus, "and if you

join us now, we
will make sure
you do well in the
days to come."

Antony shook
hands with the
conspirators, one
by one, feeling
Caesar's blood still
wet and sticky on
their fingers.

"May I speak
at the funeral?"
he asked. "If the people know I'm on
your side, they'll be less likely to
cause trouble."

"That's a good idea," said Brutus,
relieved to have won over Antony so easily.

But Cassius pulled him
to one side.

"I don't trust Antony,"
he hissed. "He's planning
something."

"Cassius, you worry too
much," Brutus said. Then
he called over to Antony, "Do you swear
that you will not say a word against us?"

"On my honour," said Antony and
he watched the conspirators head off
towards the Forum.

When at last he was alone with
Caesar's body, he fell to his knees
before it.

"Oh my dear old
friend, forgive me!" he said.
"I had to do that or they
would have killed me too.

Cry havoc, and
let slip the dogs
of war!
– Antony

But I swear that they will pay. There will be war in Rome, and I will not rest until every one of them is dead."

Word of Caesar's murder had spread quickly through the city. The Forum was already full. The crowd was in an ugly mood, spoiling for a fight.

"My friends, please!" cried Brutus. "I know you are upset. Caesar was a good man and a great general. I loved him as much as any of you. But I love Rome more! If we hadn't stopped Caesar, he would have become a tyrant and made all of us his slaves! Did I do wrong? Here is the dagger I killed him with. Only say the word and I will kill myself with it too!"

For a moment there was silence. Then the crowd spoke as one. "Live, Brutus, live!" they chanted.

"Here comes Antony with Caesar's body," Brutus went on, "you all know how close he was to Caesar, but even he has realized that we did the right thing. Antony, you wanted to speak. I will leave you here with the people."

Brutus left the Forum.

"Friends, Romans, countrymen," said Antony. "I know that Caesar had many faults. Brutus and the others say he wanted to become a tyrant, and I'm sure Brutus wouldn't lie. Of course, you will all remember the many kind things Caesar did. You'll remember the money he gave you. The food he handed out when times were hard. But Brutus says he wanted to become a tyrant, and Brutus wouldn't lie."

As he was valiant, I honour him; but as he was ambitious, I slew him
– *Brutus*

Antony kept his
promise. His words did
not directly accuse Brutus
and the others, but the
way he said them made
it clear that he thought

He was my friend,
faithful and just to me.
But Brutus says he was
ambitious; And Brutus
is an honourable man.
                – Antony

they had done something terrible. Soon
there was angry muttering in the crowd.
"Here is Caesar's will," Antony said,

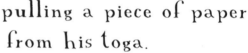

pulling a piece of paper
from his toga.
"It says that all the
great gardens he owned
in the city are to be
made into parks for
the people to enjoy.
But Brutus says
Caesar wanted to
become a tyrant,
and I'm sure he
wouldn't lie."

"Death to Brutus!" shouted someone.

"No, he is my dear friend!" said Antony. He reached into Caesar's coffin and pulled out the cloak Caesar had been wearing. "Though look at these holes that his dagger made when Brutus and the rest murdered their dear friend Caesar!"

By now, the crowd was in uproar.

"Hang the traitors!" cried one man.

"And burn down their houses!" cried another.

And the crowd swept out of the Forum, bent on revenge.

Civil War
Act four

That night, Rome blazed with fire and riot. Brutus and Cassius managed to escape before the crowd reached them. As they fled the city, they knew their only hope was to raise an army and face Antony in battle. Back in Rome, Antony summoned Caesar's heir, Octavius. Together, he thought, they would be powerful enough to defeat the conspirators. And if they won, they would be able to divide the whole Roman world between them.

In the weeks that followed, Brutus and Cassius travelled far and wide trying to recruit soldiers for their battle.

But Antony was a famous general and many people were too frightened to face him.

Cassius became convinced that Antony would defeat them and that made him very bad-tempered. He got angry at the slightest thing Brutus said and often argued with him in front of their troops.

One day in far-off Sardis, Brutus finally snapped. He wasn't going to have another fight in front of everyone, so he marched into his tent and beckoned Cassius to follow.

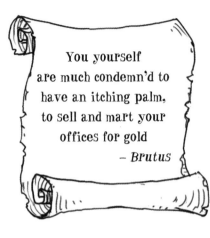

You yourself are much condemn'd to have an itching palm, to sell and mart your offices for gold

— Brutus

"Your bad temper is making the soldiers nervous," Brutus growled. "If they see us disagreeing, they'll think we won't be able to lead them in battle!"

"What do you expect me to do?" said Cassius. "You've just accused me of taking bribes!"

"Accused you?" said Brutus. "You're famous for it!"

"If anyone else said that to me," spat Cassius, "I would kill him for it!"

"We killed Caesar to preserve our honour as honest Romans," said Brutus, "and now you're taking money from all and sundry — it's disgusting!"

"Watch yourself," said Cassius. "I'm a better soldier than you!"

"Then act like one!" said Brutus.

"If only Antony were here now!" said Cassius. "He could take his revenge on me and I wouldn't even fight him. That's how sick I am of being criticized all the time!"

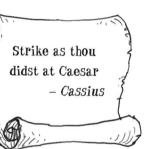

Strike as thou didst at Caesar
  – Cassius

He drew his sword and gave it to Brutus. "Come on. If I'm so bad why don't you just kill me, like you killed Caesar?"

"Stop it, please," said Brutus. "I'm sorry, Cassius."

Cassius sighed. "I'm sorry, too," he said.

Brutus fell wearily into his chair. "I've just had some very bad news," he said. "My wife Portia is dead."

"What?" said Cassius.

"She'd always been frail. When she heard Antony and Octavius had become allies, she took poison," Brutus explained.

"But that's terrible!" said Cassius.

Before Brutus could say anything, a young officer called Messala came in.

"Antony and Octavius are on the move," he said. "The reports say their armies are marching on Philippi, two hundred miles northwest of here. I've also had word that they have just executed a hundred senators in Rome – for the crime of supporting us."

"The monsters!" muttered Cassius.

"Should we go and meet the enemy at Philippi?" asked Brutus.

"No," said Cassius, "let them come and find us here. The extra march will tire them out; they'll be short of food too. We will have the advantage."

"You have a point, Cassius," said Brutus, "but the people between here and Philippi are not loyal to us. They're sure to join Antony's armies and swell his numbers. And men are already starting to desert from our ranks. We will never be more powerful than we are today. This is our moment and we must seize it while we can."

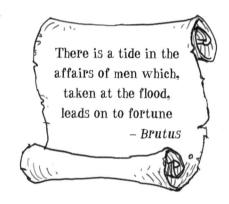

There is a tide in the affairs of men which, taken at the flood, leads on to fortune
– *Brutus*

Cassius thought a while and nodded.

"No more delays, then," he said. "We'll finish this at Philippi. Goodnight, my friend. I'm sorry I spoke so angrily to you."

"I'm sorry too," said Brutus. "Now go and get some sleep."

Try as he might, Brutus couldn't sleep that night. He ordered his servant to play soothing music for him, but the lullaby sent the servant to sleep, not Brutus!

For many hours Brutus sat alone, lost in thought, until, by the flickering light of his dying lamp, he thought he saw a man approach. Brutus looked closer. It was Caesar's ghost!

"W-w-what are you doing here?" Brutus stammered. "Why have you come?"

"To warn you," said Caesar's ghost. "You will see me again at Philippi."

"Very well then," said Brutus, feeling braver now. But before he could speak again, the ghost vanished.

Brutus rubbed his eyes and called for a guard.

"Send word to Cassius," he said, "we march for Philippi!"

Philippi

Act five

Octavius was delighted when he heard that the army of Brutus and Cassius was approaching Philippi.

"You said they wouldn't be so rash," he said to Antony. "We've got them just where we want them."

Antony was reading a letter. "They want a chance to talk before the battle," he said.

"What?" said Octavius in disbelief.

"It is the honourable thing to do," said Antony firmly, "so we will do it."

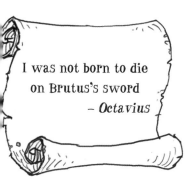

Antony and Octavius rode out to meet Brutus and Cassius in the centre of the great field. In the distance, behind them on either side, their armies stood ready for battle.

"Words before battle," said Brutus. "It's a good tradition."

"It is if you'd rather talk than fight," sneered Octavius.

"Good words are better than violent acts," said Brutus.

"What, like the good words you said to Caesar, even as you were stabbing him to death!" snapped Antony.

Octavius drew his sword.
"I'm not putting this away
again till I have avenged
all thirty-three of Caesar's
wounds and slaughtered
every one of you traitors."

"We are not traitors," said
Brutus. "We killed a tyrant
for the sake of Rome."

"Look at you two," sneered Cassius.
"A bad-tempered boy and an old drunk."

"This conversation is over," said
Octavius and he turned and rode away.
Brutus and Cassius rode back to their
positions behind the lines of their army.

As he got ready to fight, Cassius nudged Messala. "Today is my birthday," he said.

"Happy birthday," said Messala.

"Let's hope it is happy," said Cassius. "You know I've always hated superstition," he said, "but today I'm not so sure. Two mighty eagles followed our army all the way here – and the eagle is the symbol of Rome, don't forget. I looked for them this morning but they had flown away, leaving only ravens and crows overhead. I think good fortune has deserted us too."

"It's time to begin," said Brutus.

"If we are defeated, I'm not going to be taken back to Rome in chains," said Cassius.

"Nor I," said Brutus. "So today we will either triumph or die."

Our army lies ready to give up the ghost
– *Cassius*

"If this is to be our last goodbye, my dear friend," said Cassius, "then a thousand times farewell."

The two men embraced, then gave the order to attack.

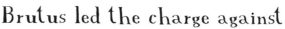

For ever and for ever, farewell, Brutus! If we do meet again, we'll smile indeed
– Cassius

Brutus led the charge against Octavius's troops. At first it was a great success, and the young man's soldiers were driven back. But Cassius's men were no match for Antony's, and soon Cassius had to flee or risk being captured.

Cassius found himself riding towards a band of mounted soldiers. He couldn't be sure whose side they were on so he sent one of his officers, Titinius, to find out.

The soldiers surrounded
Titinius, and appeared
to drag him down
from his horse. As
he disappeared from
Cassius's view, the
soldiers cheered.

"They've killed him!"
Cassius cried, panicking. He
jumped off his horse and gave his
sword to one of his slaves. "If you
want your liberty, set me free," he
said. "Kill me now and you are
a free man."

The stunned slave did
as he was told, stabbing
Cassius and then fleeing.

"Caesar, you
are revenged,"
Cassius
whispered,
and died.

But just then
Titinius returned.
The troops
surrounding Titinius
hadn't attacked him
– they'd embraced
him! When they cheered,
it was to celebrate Brutus's
success in the battle!

"Oh, Cassius, what
have you done?"
cried Titinius.

When Brutus heard
the news he was heart-
broken, but he had no
time to mourn his friend.
Instead, he led another
charge, but this time it
was beaten back and his
army was scattered. He led
a few of his closest allies
away from the battlefield.

The sun of Rome
is set
– Titinius

"My friends, you must go
before it is too late," he told
them. "Find some safe place far
away from Antony and Octavius, for
they are the masters of Rome now."

"We can't just leave you here,"
said one of his soldiers.

"You must, that is an order,"
Brutus replied.

Reluctantly, the soldiers said
farewell to their commander. As the last
of them was leaving, Brutus stopped him.

"There is one more task you can
do for me," said Brutus. He gave the
soldier his sword.

"Hold this and point it at me," he said.

The soldier knew what Brutus meant to do, and that he had no choice but to obey.

There were tears in his eyes as Brutus embraced him and the sword slid into his belly.

"Rest now, Caesar," Brutus murmured as he died.

When Antony and Octavius found Brutus's body, all their previous hatred fell away.

"He died like a soldier," said Octavius. "Too proud to be taken prisoner."

Caesar, now be still:
I killed not thee with
half so good a will
    – Brutus

"He was a man of honour,"
said Antony. "The only one of the
conspirators who killed Caesar for
Rome's sake rather than his own.
He was the noblest Roman of them all."

"Then we will give him a glorious
funeral," said Octavius. He and Antony
looked at one another. They had
triumphed, and were now the masters of
the world, but neither had ever felt so sad.

The end

Consultant: Dr Tamsin Badcoe
Editors: Ruth Symons and Carly Madden
Designer: Andrew Crowson
QED Project Designer: Rachel Lawston
Editorial Director: Victoria Garrard
Art Director: Laura Roberts-Jensen

Copyright © QED Publishing 2015

First published in the UK in 2015 by
QED Publishing
A Quarto Group company
The Old Brewery
6 Blundell Street
London N7 9BH

www.qed-publishing.co.uk

A catalogue record for this book is available from
the British Library.

ISBN 978 1 78493 006 6

Printed in China